Robotastic!

by Sari Karplus

Printed in the United States of America
First Printing, 2020
Illustrations customized by Sari Karplus
Original images used under license from shutterstock.com

ISBN 978-0-578-80893-2
www.RobotasticBook.com

For Jenny and Lindsey

Whirling his way,
through life every day.
Poor Alf was secretly sad.

No playmate in tow.
No party to throw.
Alf wanted a buddy so bad.

He used his one wish—
His BIG birthday wish!
To ask the powers that be...

"What would it take to get me a friend?
An awesome BEST FRIEND just for me!"

Not wanting to wait
Or leave it to fate
Alf had a great plan that he hatched.

He looked on the 'net,
To find his best bet:
To MAKE a new friend from scratch.

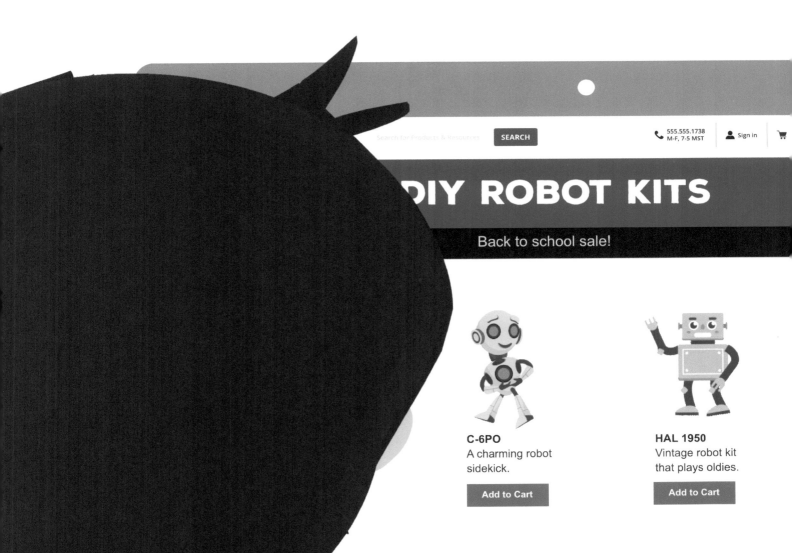

Arriving that fall,
His box was so tall!
Couldn't wait for the fun to begin!

Alf snuck that big box—
Sly as a fox—
To his room, where he could dive in.

So... Bit by bit, and byte by byte,
He built his robot kit.

Alf was having so much fun,
He didn't want to quit.

Alf named his bot "Max."
And taught him some facts
Of what a best friend should do.

Play ball and be silly,

Tell jokes willy nilly,
But always be honest and true.

Why was the robot mad?
Because you pushed its buttons.

Things started to turn,
When Alf came to learn...

That Max was confused by A HUG.

The robot asked frankly.

Alf set out to fix this weird bug.

So... Bit by bit and byte by byte,
Alf programmed Max for caring.

He gave the bot a little heart,
And taught him about sharing.

This is the coolest thing!

Alf's dad exclaimed with glee.

His mom just shook her head in awe.

I totally agree!

With the help of
both his parents,
Alf made a video.

Of boy and bot a' dancing...
And VIRAL it would go!

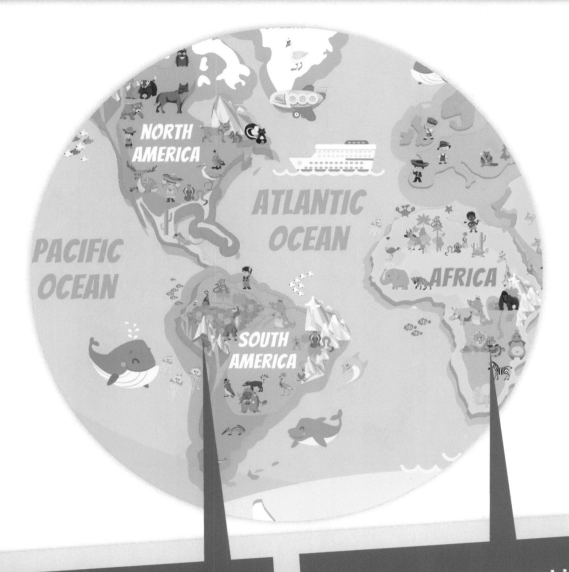

Daphne from Peru
Wants a robot unicorn.

Malcolm from Zambia
Wants a robo-dog named "Zorn."

PACIFIC OCEAN

INDIAN OCEAN

AUSTRALIA

Mina from Japan
Wants a robot that is cute.

Calvin from Australia
Wants a robot that can toot.

Alf was so excited,
By all the fun requests!

But the work ahead just too much—
He started to get stressed.

A big fan of the project—
Was a boy named Jake from Maine.

He'd seen Alf's silly video
And had a builder's brain.

Jake had no summer plans
And no bestie for himself.

Their parents had the perfect plan
So Jake could come help Alf.

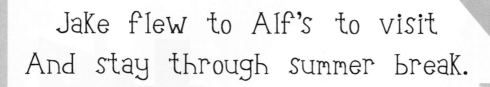

Jake flew to Alf's to visit
And stay through summer break.

Just like a two kid robo-camp,
they had a TON to make.

So... Bit by bit and byte by byte,
They put on screws and gears.

They even built a robotastic bot
With bunny ears.

They made a robot unicorn!
And taught it magic tricks.

And then they made a robo-dog,
And taught it doggy licks.

They'd giggle during breaks and munch PB&J.

Their friendship growing stronger
with each and every day.

But when the time had come...
they'd finished their endeavor.

200 robots now complete!
GREATEST. SUMMER. EVER.

Jake had to go back home,
To start school in the fall.

Since long goodbyes are oh so sad—
Their bots began to bawl.

So... Bit by bit and byte by byte,
The best thing they created...

Their very first best HUMAN friend.

Alf's wish come true— belated!

CPSIA information can be obtained
at www.ICGtesting.com
Printed in the USA
LVHW072045201220
674641LV00002B/19